Pablito Bandito

#2 The Case of the Missing Chickens

by Tomi Hall

Illustrated by Mar Cholula & Tomi Hall

ISBN: 978-1-7365785-2-0

To Selina and Nene
It's your chickens and Katie that started me
thinking of this story.

CONTENTS

Chapter 1. THE NEXT GENERATION 1

Chapter 2. SCENE OF THE CRIME 9

Chapter 3. MEETING THE NEW NEIGHBORS 15

Chapter 4. TWO NEW PROBLEMS 21

Chapter 5. THE JEEP 27

Chapter 6. IZZY'S RATTY PLANS 33

Chapter 7. IZZY STARTS TROUBLE 39

Chapter 8. IZZY'S SQUIRRELLY PLANS 43

Chapter 9. SURVEILLANCE REPORT 47

Chapter 10. THE REAL PLAN 51

Chapter 11. THE MISSION 55

Chapter 12. THE AFTER-EFFECTS 61

ABOUT THE AUTHOR 64

ACKNOWLEDGMENTS

A book isn't a solo event. It takes many people doing their parts to bring it to you, the readers. I wish to thank my Beta Readers, Bonnie and Jen, for their invaluable help. Great appreciation is due to my editor, Carol, who makes me a better writer. I'm grateful to Mar who put up with my constant changes on the artwork and listened to me read and reread sections frequently. Finally, to Miss Leonetta who read the final edit and still found things to correct. Without your help, this book wouldn't have happened. Thanks!

CHAPTER 1
THE NEXT GENERATION

I looked around at the eager young faces. Their bills all pointed to me, their attention was focused, it was time to teach the newest generation.

"For those of you who don't know me," I began, "my name is Pablo. I am the General in charge here at this farm. You can call me,

**Pablito Bandito
The Fastest Chihuahua in the Midwest!"**

"Really?" said one. The ducklings were in total awe.

"A General?" squeaked a second.

"The fastest?" quacked another.

"How is that possible?" the smallest remarked.

Humbly, I went on, "Well, I don't like to tell, but my soldiers and I have been in several battles here and at some neighboring farms, and those dogs have elected me as leader over the entire area. My great military planning and memorization of procedures, not to mention my speed, has led us to solve all kinds of problems that our humans and others get into."

"Ooh," quacked some.

"Wow," quacked others.

"But how did you get to be the fastest?" asked little Dylan Duck.

A smile came over my face as I remembered that day. "Kerrie signed me up for Chihuahua races near here. I kept winning and finally went to the Midwest finals. I won that, too, receiving a blue ribbon for first place."

"Wow!" they all quacked, their faces lighting up at my superior athleticism.

As I looked over Daisy's new flock, I realized that this is my calling: to inspire the next generation to greatness through service. The fact that I was their leader was just a cherry on the top of the ice cream.

"We have an interesting network between the farms and, when necessary, can call on each other for backup in any military conflict that presents itself. A couple of months back, we received a new mailman who didn't follow mailman rules; we had to deal with him rather severely. My troops rose to the occasion and dispatched the problem with little fanfare."

Just then, a voice piped up, "Pablo, how long have you been living on this farm?" Dylan Duck asked. "And what is that thing over your eye?"

"I've been here a long time, Dylan, enough that I know the inner workings of this farm down to the minutest detail. And this," I pointed to my eye patch, "is the result of our last war. I was shot and have a permanent scar to show for it. War isn't pretty, kids; we have to take the good with the bad. The most important thing is that we rescued our former mailman, Gene, and now he works full-time at the farm with us."

"Wow, you are amazing," Dylan said.

"Yeah, cool too," the rest of them murmured.

I find talking with the youngsters on the farm refreshing. It is lonely at the top and explaining procedures or giving our farm's history brings me peace.

Suddenly Wonton and Bobby ran up to us. "Permission to speak freely, Sir?" Wonton asked.

"Let's step away from little ears," I remarked. We moved to the back of the duck barnyard, and I turned to the two.

"Okay, give it to me straight. What is the problem?"

"We just did our security rounds, and upon meeting up with Rover and Roger from the next farm, we found out that their chickens have gone missing. One was left, and the poor thing is scared out of her mind. She said big monster dogs came and took the other ladies away. The twins mentioned their coop was a mess with feathers everywhere."

"This is serious. You two get back to the twins, and I'll secure our farm. Give Roger and Rover whatever they need. Do you want me to send more soldiers over?" I asked.

"We will report back to you in an hour with their needs," Wonton replied over her shoulder as the two trotted back to Bob's farm.

"Daisy and kids, I'm sorry, but I will not be taking you down to see the pond today to talk over swimming safety. We seem to have a little problem that needs my attention at the next farm over. To make sure you are safe, I want you to shelter in place here at your barnyard."

I could see the fear in the small ducks' faces, but they had to know it just wasn't safe for them to go out.

"Will you stay with us, Pablo?" Dylan pleaded.

"No, I must go get my troops, and we must take care of the problem, young one. Stay close to your mom, and you will be fine."

"Pablo, are you sure?" Daisy appealed. "I would feel safer if you or one of your soldiers could be with us."

"Fine, I will send one back to you. I don't want you to be upset." I then sprinted to the kennel yard, yelling orders all the way to Izzy.

When I got to her, I yelled, "Izzy, did you hear what I said?" as I watched her twirling around.

"Well, no, you were running, and I was twirling. It pretty much came out like gobbledygook," Izzy answered. "Have you seen my ball, ball, ball while you were running?"

"No time for balls, Izzy. We have a serious problem. You go to Daisy and take care of her and the ducklings.

Do not leave them until I have either fixed the problem or sent you a replacement."

"Okay, Boss," said Izzy, twirling around and around.

"Stop twirling and go, Izzy!" I yelled.

"Okay, I'm going, going, going," she yelled as she ran towards the duck barn.

"Recruits, gather round!" I called to the rest of my squad. "We have a serious problem. The chickens at the twins' farm were all kidnapped last night except one. She is seriously traumatized and can't give much of a description of what happened. Lexy, head over to their farm and see if you can get more info from her. Izzy has gone to guard our ducks. Cap and Nala, start a perimeter check immediately. Report back every hour. The rest of you do security here on the farm. No one in or out unless you know them."

My soldiers jumped into action as I called to Sophie and our new dog Sydnie. I haven't had time to analyze Sydnie enough to know her total strengths, since she just arrived the day before yesterday. As a border collie/husky mix, she tended toward the border collie in most of her actions, but I did notice that the instinct to kill is in her eyes. I might need to pull that husky trait out if this mission gets messy.

"Sophie, you and Sydnie head down the drive and wait for Gene. Bring him to me as soon as he arrives. We are going to have to get him up to speed. We may need his help with this mission." Since we rescued him, our former mailman works for Mom now. He is a retired Marine and knows procedures and mission planning almost as well as me. It will be great to have him aboard this next mission.

After everyone went to their places, I ran into the house, checking under the table to see if I had missed any tidbits left by the kids from breakfast. With my soldiers doing their jobs, I thought I could take a small nap to energize myself for the next part of the operation.

CHAPTER 2
SCENE OF THE CRIME

I awoke, got a drink, and wandered outside. I was refreshed and ready to give the problem of the missing chickens my all. Just then, I noticed Sophie and Sydnie coming up the driveway with Gene.

"Gene, good to see you, we have a situation here," I said.

"Pablo, what has your knickers in such a wad?"

"That's what I'm trying to tell you. Geez, listen to me, man, I'm the General!"

"How about you show me?" Gene suggested.

The four of us walked over to the next farm, where Gene found out from the owner, Bob, that some chickens were missing. They were talking about who and why, so my team and I went to the coop to see if we could get more information.

"There you guys are," I mentioned to the twins and my three fighters when we found them. They were sitting in a large circle with their backs to the chicken coop. "Excellent formation, guards," I barked, very impressed that they had set up the perimeter of the coop without my instructions. Perhaps they, at least, were learning from me.

"Stay here for the night, soldiers, and I'll send over replacements tomorrow. No sleeping. I want this last chicken to have the best security. Lexy, did you learn anything from her?"

"Yes, actually, she indicated that it was three men who made off with her friends, not three dogs or coyotes."

"Men, you say? Well, that is unusual. Let's go back to the house and let Gene know."

We said our goodbyes to Wonton, Bobby, Roger and Rover. With Lexy, we headed back over to Gene and Bob. As we trotted, I realized that humans have a horrible habit of hurting the weak. It was not right, and in the case of the chickens, something I was going to fix.

Gene was just saying goodbye to Bob, but I wanted him to know that we had the security set up. Leading both men back to the coop, they could immediately see that I had taken care of the safety of the lonesome hen. How her world had been rocked today, I expected some PTSD coming on soon. The stress was already showing on her face.

"Good job, Pablo," Gene said. "I see you have security tight for tonight. Bob, I think these two will stay through the night with your boys, and we can assure your last chicken won't get attacked by the wild dogs."

I started yelling, "It's not dogs! It's men!"

"Pablo, I see you have your troops in place. Quiet down now," Gene said to me.

Goodness, he really wasn't listening to me. Maybe he needs one of those hearing aids I see on TV. I understand from the commercials that older people have this problem all the time. Maybe there was a free study we could get him in.

"I'll also run over to the Anderson farm and let them know," Gene said to Bob as we walked down the path to the road.

"The Anderson family moved out last month, and new people have moved in already. From what I hear, they are just renting the place. Oddly, it is on a month-to-month basis," Bob replied. "That just doesn't seem right for farmers."

"Huh, that is weird," Gene muttered. "I think it might be a good time to go introduce myself and get a feel for them. If we all work together, we can get the coyotes to move on."

"Let me know what you find out, Gene," Bob stated as we started walking back down the road. "Those coyotes need to go; plus, I'm going to have to get more chickens too."

I looked up at Gene and again started telling him that it was people, not dogs, not coyotes. But still, he continued to shush me. "Yep, I'm going to have to see about getting you a hearing aid," I mumbled to myself.

CHAPTER 3
MEETING THE NEW NEIGHBORS

After we walked back home, Gene checked in with Mom and then whistled to me.

"Come on, Pablo, we will go visit the new folks at the Anderson farm. Time to make some introductions and let them know what's up."

We drove down to the next farm and pulled in close to the house. Something made the hairs on my back stand up. I couldn't have told you what it was, but I sensed that Gene felt it too.

"Stick close to me, Pablo. We don't know these people yet, so we need to give them our best face forward." I knew what he meant, but I wasn't getting a good feeling.

Three men walked out of the house when we started up the pathway. They were not at all friendly, which was evident from the looks on their faces.

"Hi, gentlemen, I'm Gene. I'm from the next farm over and wanted to come to meet you."

He shook hands all around. Weirdly they didn't mention their names.

"And this is my assistant, Pablo." I put my paw up to shake hands, but no one shook. That didn't sit well with me. Manners and proper due respect are everything in my book, after all I am the General.

"I wanted to let you know that we seem to have some coyotes wreaking havoc on our farms right now. They are most likely enlarging their territory but unfortunately, got most of the chickens at Bob Fredrick's farm just down the road from us. Have you had any problems?"

"Nope," the older man answered. "Thanks for stopping by and telling us. We will be on the watch for the coyotes. We don't have any farm animals yet, but we will keep a lookout." And with that, they turned and started to go back into the house.

The hair on my neck went up when they tried to blow us off. I walked up to the older man and took a big sniff. I caught a familiar whiff. Where had I smelled that scent before?

I decided to check out the other two, but one of the men nudged me away with his foot. "Gene," I hollered, "he is trying to kick me!"

I was catching a smell of them now, my nose on high alert. It unsettled me, and I kept yelling to Gene, "I know this scent - something isn't right here."

Gene grabbed me and walked back to the truck. He didn't hurry though, as a Marine never walks scared.

When we were in the truck, I looked Gene straight in the eye and started in, "I don't like them. There is something…I can't put my paw on it, but I don't trust them. They are not nice people."

"Well, Little Man, you don't seem impressed with the new neighbors either," Gene said. "I think I need to do some checking up on them. Something isn't sitting right with me. Think I'll call Sheriff Tenny and have a chat."

"Me either," I barked and settled into the passenger seat. I liked riding in the truck but would rather be driving it.

"Zeke used to have a small kid jeep in the garage. That would be perfect for me to drive around. I'm going to learn to drive it." I mentioned to Gene.

"Sounds good, Pablo," Gene said.

Wahoo, Gene agreed with me learning to drive! Do you see why I love this guy?

When we got back home, I ran over to the squad.

"I have a bad feeling about the new neighbors; something is not right," I told the team. "They aren't friendly, like super not friendly. One even tried to kick me. There were no females there, and I also caught a scent I've smelled before. It is bugging me, but I just can't put my paw on where I sniffed it before."

Izzy started twirling around, "Cap will know, Cap will know, Cap will know." She was right, Cap is part basset hound and has the best scent nose at the farm.

"Good idea, Izzy. Prepare for a mission, soldiers; we have some neighbors to watch tonight. Best if we get in a good nap. We will be busy later."

Chapter 4
Two New Problems

After supper, I pretended to go to bed and fall asleep. When Mom called me from my kitchen bed to come upstairs, I didn't react and just kept lying there. She finally shrugged her shoulders and went upstairs without me.

Shortly after midnight, I heard, "Psst, psst, psst" in my ear. It was Izzy.

"What?" I mumbled without opening my eyes.

"Come on, we need to go check out the new, new, new neighbors."

"Right, I was thinking up our strategy as I was lying here."

"Okay, if you say so, but it looked like you were sleeping, sleeping, sleeping to me," Izzy replied.

"Well, I never," I started saying, but decided I didn't need to confront her with her insolence at this moment.

Outside, Cap and Lexy were waiting. "Lexy, I think it would be best if you guard the ducks while we go."

Lexy has two back legs that don't work well on long runs. She has had several surgeries on them and just didn't have the endurance this mission required.

"Good idea, General," Lexy replied and walked off to the duck barn.

"Cap, Izzy, let's go."

We started running and running. Phew, I really need to get that jeep going. I was beginning to get winded. Cap and Izzy looked fine, though.

I had put on a couple of ounces since my eye injury. "Note to self: exercise starting tomorrow and find the jeep."

We stayed in the shadows when we reached the Anderson farm driveway. Skirting the tree line, we silently sneaked up to the house.

"Wait," Cap whispered. "I'm catching the scent--maybe, wait, no," and he veered off to the barn.

"Cap, what are you doing?" Izzy muttered.

"Come with me; something isn't right," Cap answered. We followed Cap and came upon a small barn. Staying back, we looked over the barn.

"There is something in that barn that we need to check out, I can smell it." Cap finally said.

While we all sat and thought about what Cap said, Izzy got tired of waiting for us to move, so she ran to a hole she spotted at the bottom of the barn. She poked her head through and then the rest of her body followed.

"Come on," Izzy whispered back to us. After we both squeezed in after her, Cap slowly led us steadily down rows of cow stalls. Just then he stopped and haltingly looked around the corner. I instantly smelled fear and aggressive training.

Loud growls from around that corner made us turn and run out of the barn, but not before I picked up another scent--the smell of chickens!

We ran back to our farm as fast as we could, checking behind us often to see if we were being followed. Thankfully we weren't. We went straight to the water bowl, taking long drinks to rehydrate ourselves.

"That was weird," I said. "What were those growls from?"

"Those growls, my General, were from two Dobermanns," Cap answered. "But what is even more interesting is that behind them were crates stuffed with chickens. And not any chickens, but the chickens from Bob's farm!"

"I knew it!" I yelled. That was where I caught that scent. It was those three men. I smelled it while I was at Bob's farm by the chicken coop.

"Wow!" Izzy jumped. "Didn't see that coming, coming, coming. Are you sure, you guys?"

"The General's nose never lies, and my eyesight is good, even in a dark barn," Cap answered.

"This is a big problem. The people thought it was coyotes that took the chickens, but it was the new neighbors," I stated. "Soldiers, I need time to plan our next mission. We must rescue these chickens, but we have two worthy adversaries that are protecting them. Let's get a good night's sleep, and I'll have a plan by morning."

CHAPTER 5
THE JEEP

I awoke with an idea. Running to the kitchen to scrounge for food, I realized that Fruity Circles are not my favorite cereal but will do in a pinch when I'm hungry. After breakfast, I went out to the kennel yard to gather the troops.

"Company, it is all hands-on deck. We found out what happened to the chickens. They are being held hostage at the Anderson farm."

The gasps from the crew echoed across the yard.

"First, has anyone seen Zeke's old jeep he used to drive around in?"

"What, what, what," yelled Izzy, "does that have to do with saving the chickens?"

"Once again, Izzy, don't interrupt me. Besides, I have a plan."

"Plan, schman, those dogs have to sleep sometime, let's go!" Izzy yelled.

I heard mumbling throughout the ranks. I had to stop it immediately.

"Battalion!" I yelled sharply. "We found the chickens and have to rescue them without the possibility of injury to them or to ourselves. There are two Dobermanns guarding the chickens, which have been trained to be mean. I will not put you in danger if I can help it."

"Good point," the company conceded, "but what are we going to do?"

"Recognizance," I said. "We are going to divide the team up and watch the barn tonight. There are plenty of trees to hide behind, and we can learn a lot in a few hours."

"Private Nala, I have a special project for you. Please come with me for further instructions."

"Bobby and Wonton, get Rover and Roger. Let Bob know that you are bringing the last chicken with you. Put her in with the ducks."

"Lexy and Cap, I need you to guard them all."

"Sydnie and whoever is left, go find Gene. I want you all back here in 20 minutes."

As I walked away, I felt the team getting stronger from my decisive directions. Izzy tried to stir up a problem, but my leadership squelched it and put them all on the proper course.

Twenty minutes later, my soldiers were all assembled, including Gene. Nala and I were behind the patio. I was standing in the jeep with my camo hat placed perfectly on my head and a bulletproof vest securely on my body.

With Nala at the pedals and me leaning against the horn by the dashboard, we slowly started driving the jeep towards the team -- what a glorious entrance. Perfect for a General of my stature.

There was, however, a slight malfunction, and the jeep didn't drive straight. I sort of ended up crashing up into the side of the deck. I had to jump out, but all my soldiers got the idea that I was driving and in complete charge of this operation. I should take a bow.

Gene started laughing. "Pablo, you are a riot. Where did you get that little jeep? Who is driving it?" Nala stuck her head out from under my seat and jumped out, dusting herself off. She had a big grin on her face.

"Well, you are going to have to learn to steer the wheel if you are going to get anywhere with that plan." Gene continued while still laughing.

"What wheel? There are four of them," I said, definitely confused, but Nala and I would figure it out later. My entrance was just as I had planned – epic!

"Soldiers, we are going to take three shifts. I want 24 hours of eyes on the Anderson farm, Sydnie and Rover, you are first. Leave now."

The two of them trotted out and headed off.

"Roger and Bobby, second shift," and they looked up at the sun to gauge their time.

"Wonton and Nala, third shift." They too checked the sun so they would know when to leave.

"Remember there are two Dobermanns that are guarding the chickens, we must be careful and not let them know we are there. Stay upwind from them so they can't catch your scent which would give away your positions. Fall out troops!"

Each of the regiment ran to their posts and Gene smiled at me. "So, a little surveillance, huh, Pablo? A good idea, my man."

But Gene didn't see what I had seen. Izzy was sneaking out of the yard running after Sydnie and Rover.

Chapter 6
Izzy's Ratty Plans

Izzy ran as fast as she could. Within two minutes she had caught up with Sydnie and Rover.

"Did Pablo ask you to join us?" Rover asked.

"No, but I have another idea to help us, and it's going to have to come from me," Izzy replied. "I want to ask some very important critters to help us out, but we don't have the best relationship, and it will take a delicate hand to convince them."

"What are you talking about, Izzy?" Sydnie asked.

"The chickens are penned up in crates. The only way to get them out of the crates is to send in rats that will chew a chicken-sized hole in the crates."

"Oh, I get it, Izzy," said Sydnie. "But you are a rat terrier. You kill rats. How are you going to get them to help you?"

"Well, that's the little problem I have with this plan. I'm not at all liked by the rat population."

"Show me where the rats are, and I'll try and get them to help," Sydnie said.

"What makes you think you can talk them into it?" Rover asked.

"A background of convincing sheep to do as they are asked," Sydnie said, winking.

"Sounds good to me, me, me," Izzy answered. 'All three sat in place by the barn the chickens were being held in. Izzy, very alert, was looking around the barn and the farm. The other two watched Izzy to wait for her detection of the rats.

"Aha!" she finally said. "Sydnie, there is a hole at the back corner of the barn. It is away from where they said the Dobermanns are. Straight out from that corner is a pile of rubbish. Do you see it?"

"Yes," Sydnie said.

"Well, that is where the rats are," said Izzy. Sydnie watched and soon they all saw the rats slipping in and out of the barn and running to the pile.

"Be right back; wish me luck," Sydnie said as she crept to get into position.

"I've never seen her work before," said Rover, "but she certainly has some skills. Look at her getting close up on those rats without them seeing her."

Sydnie crept closer and closer until she was at the opening of the rat pile. She quietly whispered to the pile, "I want to talk with your leader."

"Who do you think you are, asking us such a thing?" Two beady eyes looked out at her.

"I'm here to make you a proposition. One that will reward you with better food."

A very large male rat stuck his head out of the pile. "Who are you and what do you have to offer?"

"I'm Sydnie from the next farm over. Some chickens have been kidnapped and are being held here in the barn."

"Yeah, we know, so what?" Beady answered.

"They belong to friends of ours and they want them back."

"Well, la di da. We all want things we can't get," Beady answered.

"That's why I'm going to make it worth your while to help us," Sydnie countered.

"How could you make it worth my while, dog?" Venom dripped from Beady's voice.

"How about fresh eggs every day for a month?" Sydnie tempted.

"How about fresh eggs for two months?" countered Beady.

"How about fresh eggs for one month with total access to our dump pile, also for a month?" responded Sydnie.

"Ummmm, how about..." Beady considered.

"That's the final offer," Sydnie said thwarting the continuation of the bargaining.

"Okay, we accept. But keep that rat terrier away from us or the deal is off."

"Sold," Sydnie said. "Now, here's what we need you to do. Go into the barn and start chewing the back of the crates the chickens are in. Make the holes big enough for them to get out quickly."

"They ain't gonna let us get near them without a racket," Beady countered.

"True. Let me get word to them before you start," Sydnie said.

"You mess with us and we will take your farm out," Beady threatened.

"No worries, pal. We won't mess with you or our agreement." Sydnie trotted away, betting herself that Beady would just continue threatening her if she stayed.

Sydnie sneaked back to Rover and Izzy, not giving away their position.

"Izzy," she said, "can you get to the back of the barn without being caught by the Dobermanns and let the chickens know the rats are going to start coming and chewing holes in the crates? They can't try and peck the rats, and they have to keep quiet with just their soft clucking so the dogs don't get suspicious."

"Be right back, back, back," said Izzy with a twirl.

She found a safe way to get back to the chickens, letting them know what to expect and how to act. "If I could chew up the crates, I'd do it myself," Izzy told them. "Just put up with the rats for a short time and we will get you out and back home, I promise."

After Izzy returned, Sydnie went and gave a signal to the rats. The rats started their comings and goings.

Chapter 7
Izzy Starts Trouble

When they returned to the farm, Sydnie, Rover, and Izzy brought me, Pablo, up to date with their plan.

"Well, my, my, you three. I really must say that is a plan. But you know you can't trust the rats! It is a wrong move, one I would never have made, but we will proceed with your plan until it fails. Next time check with me first on any strategic maneuvers. I have way more experience than you."

"Pablo, you are a big blow!" Izzy shouted. "It's a good idea and you know it. Just because you didn't think of it doesn't mean it is bad. You annoy me, big time! I'm going to go find some squirrels and have an intelligent conversation."

"You just go ahead and talk to those scatterbrains! You'll fit right in!" I screamed right back at Izzy.

Sydnie and Rover decided to go find Mom and try to get a treat out of her. There was no sense getting in between Izzy and me when we were fighting. We could keep it up for hours.

The rest of the day, I kept yelling at Izzy whenever she was near me. She had no authority to plan a mission without me and I kept letting the brainless one know that fact.

Unfortunately, my reprimanding of Izzy was not sitting well with the rest of the soldiers, especially Sydnie and Rover. They too started barking.

Gene finally came out of the kennel and whistled for us all. "Alright Pablo and Izzy, knock it off. I know you have something planned and I'm sure this disagreement has something to do with it. But your testy attitudes are upsetting the pups. Your mom is having a hard time getting them to calm down. Enough or I'm going to crate the two of you." Izzy stopped yelling immediately.

"Wait! What? No way! Crate me?" I hollered at Gene. "I am the General here! Izzy needs to know it, and you need to know it!" Gene just shrugged his head, picked me up, and carried me into the kennel. I kept yelling, but he really did stick me into the small crate and then told Mom where I was.

"Oh, I know, Gene. Pablo can get a bee in his bonnet and not drop it when he thinks he has been wronged. The only way to get him to stop is to crate him until he calms down. He will be extra cuddly when you take him out."

A while later, Gene finally came and took me out of the kennel. I snuggled up to him and planted several kisses on his chin.

"I'm okay now," I cooed. "You understand military procedures and know how tough it is when discipline and proper informational procedures are not maintained."

"Pablo let's get the plan going for tonight. I have your team calm and ready to go."

We walked with dignity back out into the yard--the two military leaders meeting with the troops. With Gene next to me, I could face my selectees without blowing up at Izzy again.

I started the instructions. "Listen up, soldiers! Same positions as last night. Watch and learn our enemies' ways. The best plan will come when we share our observations. Meet tomorrow morning after pup time and we will discuss this. Dismissed!" I yelled.

Gene smiled as the soldiers disbursed and went to their posts.

Weirdly, Izzy hadn't been at the meeting, but she was most likely hiding out licking her wounds from the tongue lashing I had given her earlier.

CHAPTER 8
IZZY'S SQUIRRELLY PLANS

Meanwhile, at the woods outside of the Anderson farm, Izzy was talking it up with the squirrels. Sydnie's way of negotiating with the rats had gotten Izzy thinking of using the squirrels, too.

She found the leader of the squirrels, Little Lady One Ear. She was the mom to so many of the squirrels in the group, and she ruled them with an iron fist.

"Little Lady, if you could get your squirrels in and out of the barn without getting the Dobes upset, we can gain valuable intel about the two dogs to help us rescue the chickens. We'll also give you a wonderful present in return for your cooperation."

"Well, Izzy, I am upset about the way they are treating the chickens. Also, those dogs haven't been let out for two days. We'll be happy to help report to your friends what's happening in the barn."

Little Lady One Ear ran away and talked with her kids. Izzy poked her head in the hole at the bottom of the barn and could see the squirrels start crawling up on the rafters to see what was happening with the Dobermanns.

All this intel would cost them was a bag of peanuts. Because Izzy knew right where one was, payment wouldn't be a problem.

This plan started working right away. Sydnie and Rover were impressed with the information they were receiving from the squirrels.

"Since Pablo insists on knowing everything, the teams will report to him in the morning, and he wouldn't go mental thinking I made a plan without him," Izzy thought.

"We will have better intel through the squirrels, and it won't cost anything for the nuts. It's a win in my book," Izzy said to herself.

Each team of dogs that came to the Anderson farm was given Izzy's directions. They received timetables of the Dobermanns, their eating habits, and even their bathroom schedules. They also gave information on how the rats were doing on completing the hole-chewing.

A younger squirrel got brave and went right up to the Dobermanns. They thought he was so stupid that they didn't pay attention to him, and he climbed up the side of the cow stall. He found something very interesting.

The Dobes were in the same cow stall as the chickens, but were separated from them by a large, heavy wire wall.

CHAPTER 9

SURVEILLANCE REPORT

The next morning, I, Pablo, called the squadron under the tree for a meeting. "Team 1, what is your report?"

Sydnie reported with Rover: "The chickens are separated from the Dobermanns by a large wire wall that extends up the entire backside of the cow stall. There is a gate to the chickens, but it has two slide bolts."

"Really interesting information. Good job, you two. Team 2, your report." Roger and Bobby stepped up to me.

"Our intelligence has revealed that the Dobermanns are not fed sufficient amounts of food. They are fed only once a day with a scoop of feed missing each time. They are both hungry and complaining frequently about not having enough to eat. They are always trying different things to get into the chickens to eat them."

"Excellent, excellent info," I replied. Starving the Dobes so they will attack whoever tries to come into the barn--a very poor way to get dedication to service, and not good for the health of the Dobes."

"Team 3, what have you learned?' I then asked Cap and Nala.

"We found that at night the dogs are let out of their cage to run around the entire barn. They use a couple of the other stalls to poop in. The younger two men are supposed to clean up after the dogs, but they aren't doing it. They just feed the chickens and complain about the older man who is their dad. Also, they are scared of the Dobes, so they have some weird ways of blocking them with the stall doors when they let them out, so they never get near them."

"Excellent, excellent, Troops. These are all things we can use for our final mission. Let's go work with the pups, and I'll come up with our final mission by tonight. Sophie, go relieve Lexy with the ducks," I said as the rest of us trotted over to the kennel to see if it was time for a treat.

Chapter 10
The Real Plan

At lunch, all the humans were sitting at the table when Gene cleared his throat. "Ecklyn, Quinn, I have been checking with Sheriff Tenny, and there seems to be some inconsistencies with the story the new folks at the Anderson farm are putting out."

"Those men told the Sheriff that they were coming from Oklahoma after the death of his wife. Only, there are no death records or any records that match up with them ever being in Oklahoma. In fact, the sheriff can't find anybody with their first and last names ever being in the United States. He is thinking they might be part of a traveling poaching group."

My ears perked up as I continued my primary mission of catching any food that fell from the table.

Mom and Dad nodded their heads, and Dad said, "That makes sense. Two other farms have reported missing chickens also. Do you guys have something planned to do?"

"The sheriff and his men, plus Bob and I, are going to go over to the farm to do some surveillance tonight. Would you like to come with us, Quinn?" Gene asked Dad.

"Yep, I think I would. I don't like when men steal from others' hard work. Let's go in hot though, we never know what thieves are packing and I don't want any surprises."

"Sheriff Tenny is going to deputize us so we can work with them, Gene added.

Once lunch was over, I decided against a nap and went to tell the troops what I had learned and how the menfolk were going to go over to the Anderson farm that night. Izzy sat quietly and listened but took off as soon as I was finished. Now what was she doing?

I followed her at a distance and noticed that Izzy had gone over to the brick pile. She sat still for several minutes before the head skunk came out. Unfortunately, Izzy has a rather sketchy history with skunks. Last summer she mistakenly killed a baby skunk, and all the other skunks took her to task for it. They had sprayed her just about every week. I could see it coming, this was going to be a disaster! She was going to get blasted by them again. Why would she even go over by them? She was going to undo the truce I had made with them.

I could still remember how mad Mom was at her for stinking up the whole farm after getting blasted so many times. That was some of the fiercest negotiations I'd ever done to get that truce. Izzy agreed not to kill any more babies and the skunks agreed to leave us alone and stop spraying. Of course, we can't sneak up on them and say "Boo" either. But it is the price we have to pay to all get along on the farm and make Mom happy.

I still wondered what Izzy was doing with the skunk. With my stealth, I sneaked a little closer, hoping to catch some of the conversation. It was weird, Izzy wasn't twirling around and all I could hear was that she was talking to the head skunk.

Just then the skunk nodded and said rather loudly, "Just let me know and my team will be there, Izzy. We are here to help."

What? Be where? What was her plan? Wait, this is Izzy, and I'm sure the skunks just agreed to another hair-brained scheme of hers. That's it! There is no doubt that she is going rogue, and so I'm going to have to get her locked up until she can respect the rules of our battalion. If she doesn't stop, I'm going to have to court-martial her and get her banned from our farm. I don't want to do it, but I can't have one of the soldiers going off on her own and causing mayhem in the ranks. After all, I am the General!

CHAPTER 11
THE MISSION

That evening, Dad, Gene and I went over to the Anderson farm before 2100 hours. I planned to extricate the chickens before the two younger men at the farm came out to feed them. Well, that was my plan but that's not how it went.

Izzy, Cap, Bobby, and Wonton were already at the farm when we arrived. "Okay," I said, "this is my plan for tonight's mission." I started to give directions, but my soldiers weren't listening to me. I growled at them.

Wonton put her paw on my shoulder and said, "Watch this, General. We took all your plans and are ready to execute them."

"Great, I look forward to seeing you in action. Wait, what plans?" I asked. "The only plan I have is to get the chickens out."

"The plans for taking down these thieves. It's brilliant, General," Wonton added.

"Hold your horses. Thank you for understanding my brilliance, but ..." Just then Sheriff Tenny and the men from the other farms arrived and started spreading out, making a perimeter between the house and where the chickens were being held.

"Troops," I said softly, "back up the sheriff's team. Let them know you are here and working with them." But my soldiers didn't advance.

Immediately, everything started moving in fast-forward. Rats started running into the back of the barn. Four of my squad ran to the back with them.

Next squirrels were going in a hole near the front of the barn. Weirdly, Nala, Cap, and Katie went in with them. Cap had to shimmy a bit, but they were all able to get in.

I couldn't bark and give away my soldiers' positions, but what was this? Who made this plan? Why weren't they waiting for me to direct them? What was going on?

Izzy gave a short bark, and the pandemonium began. The squirrels dropped down and unlatched the door of the stall the Dobes were in. The two dogs ran out, chasing other squirrels until they saw Katie dog. "Na na na na na na," she sang. The Dobes got really mad and they started to chase Katie. As a supreme athlete and gymnast, she led them into another cow stall where Nala and Katie closed the gate and the squirrels jumped up and locked them in.

The Dobes were completely focused on Katie who backed herself into a corner whimpering. Oh no, was she going to sacrifice herself for the chickens? But wait, did she have a pogo stick in her tail? Katie jumped up 8 feet and went over the wall into the next stall. The Dobes lunged at her, but they couldn't get up high enough to catch her. She ran out of the stall and joined up with her friends at the hole. They shimmied through again and joined the rats and others at the back of the barn.

I heard clucking and saw a nice straight line of chickens coming out of the back of the barn. "What?" I murmured. My regiment was forming a protective dog barrier around the chickens and walking them back to our farm.

The noise of the snarling Dobes caught the attention of the men in the Anderson house. They ran out the back door with their guns drawn. The older man started barking orders, "Larry, Wayne, go get those chickens, I'm going to get these meddling dogs. Tarnation, interrupting our supper, I've had it with them."

The sheriff, his men, my soldiers, and some of the farmhands converged on the two sons and their dad. Sheriff Tenny announced, "Police! Drop the weapons, hands up! Don't move or we'll shoot."

The three men quickly followed orders, but the sheriff and his men didn't move to cuff them.

That's when I noticed skunks were walking and surrounding the thieves. At a nod from Izzy, they all put up their tails and shot the three with their best skunk smell.

"Ohhhh, no," yelled the three men. The skunks walked away with satisfied smirks on their faces. Each of the thieves was coughing and crying and spluttering as the sheriff and his men finally put them in handcuffs.

"Ummm, if you don't mind, Sheriff, I don't want them riding to jail in my van," Deputy Lyons remarked.

All the men laughed, and Sheriff Tenny said, "Think I'll let them walk to the police station so they can air out."

"What are we going to do with those Dobes?" asked Gene. Just then Bobby ran out of the back door of the house with two big steaks in his mouth. Katie shimmied back into the barn, pulling the steaks in with her. She jumped up to the top of the stall and dropped the steaks in to the Dobes. They were occupied for at least a couple of seconds getting real food that filled their bellies properly.

CHAPTER 12
THE AFTER-EFFECTS

It was about 0300 hours when we were all back at the farm. The three men had been hosed down with a special skunk spray neutralizer and were all tucked into their beds in the jail at the police station.

Bob's wife, Marie, and Mom had sandwiches and soup all made for the men, and I was under the table getting my fill of whatever dropped.

Gene bent down to pet me on the head. "That was a masterful mission, Pablo. I couldn't have planned that better myself."

"That was the best planning I've ever seen," Sheriff Tenny added.

I was proud, too, but realized that he was praising the wrong dog. "Izzy planned it and I can't take credit," I barked.

But Gene didn't understand me and petted me again, murmuring, "Good job, Little Man."

"Note to self, check into a hearing aid for Gene tomorrow," I mumbled.

The chickens were all back in their proper coop at their farm. They too were tucked in their beds safe and sound with the dogs surrounding them. It would be some time before they recovered from their ordeal. As soon as they produced eggs again, the rats were going to have a party.

The Dobes were being housed in a special kennel on our farm for a couple of days and wouldn't be let out with the pups or us since they didn't have proper manners yet.

"The Dobes are going to be picked up by the Dobermann Rescue group Thursday," Mom said. "They have some intense rehabilitation to go through, plus just getting them up to proper weight is going to take some time. Hopefully, they will be able to be adopted into a loving family someday."

Another piece of turkey meat fell off of a sandwich and down to me. I realized I didn't want it. I was so tired and still a little confused about how Izzy planned all this without my knowledge. More importantly, she wasn't as ditzy as I thought she was. It had been a good plan. I must be rubbing off on her. I will give her a medal tomorrow and praise her to the rest of the team. She deserves their applause.

It had been an exhausting last three days, so I proceeded upstairs to the bedroom. I could still hear the muffled talk of the people downstairs. I curled myself up into a ball and settled down in my comfy bed. Tomorrow was another day, and I would find out how Izzy put this all together. But for now, I wanted to go to sleep. And so, I did.

About the Author

Tomi Hall is a retired teacher who has finally decided to write down the stories that have been in her head all these years. An advocate of finding dogs forever homes, she is kept amused by the antics of Katie, her current rescue dog. Katie likes to climb trees after squirrels and jump six-foot fences to visit her friends in the neighborhood.

About the Illustrator

Mar Cholula has been interested in drawing from an early age. She continues to hone her skills through college classes, exploring different media to expand her methods. Her followers enjoy her figures, moons, and stars, and the unique style that is found in her work. She also enjoys pottery and printmaking. Mar is influenced by Japanese pop culture and early 2000s' cartoons that focus on original characters.

Want to become a member
of my elite team of soldiers?

For updates on new releases, activities, products, giveaways, and other random stuff, sign up for my newsletter at:

www.pablitobandito.com

I also have a group on Facebook for my fans to hang out. They love my troops and are the first to find out about my new stories as well as throwing in their own ideas that sometimes make it into print!

Looking forward to talking with you there,

Pablo

www.facebook.com/Author-Tomi-Hall-Pablito-Bandito-101753645310069

Made in the USA
Monee, IL
08 July 2021